Marigold

Also by Troy James Weaver

Visions
Witchita Stories

Marigold

TROY JAMES WEAVER

A KING SHOT BOOK
Portland | Athens

FIRST KING SHOT PRESS EDITION

King Shot Press
P.O. Box 80601
Portland, OR 97280

Cover design copyright © 2016 Matthew Revert
www.matthewrevert.com
Interior design by Michael Kazepis

Portions of this book have appeared in slightly altered form in *Nailed Magazine* and *Funhouse Magazine*.

ISBN 978-0-9972518-0-7
Printed in the United States of America

For those without hope,
know the decibels through which your silence speaks

"Mythology and Cigarette Ash," a Brief Foreword

The first time I met Troy Weaver was outside a small north-western bar in the heart of a literature festival. I kept retreating to the sidewalk, like I'd been practicing holding my breath, because something about confined spaces full of people fills me with unease and it takes a while to adjust. Weaver was dressed in jeans and a black shirt, and he carried with him a folded paperback. I don't remember what he read that night, just how he read it. The cracking hurt in his voice as he disappeared into a vignette. Some writers you just feel in your blood, you know? And this is a man born to write, believe this. His work is immensely cathartic, medicinal almost, like you've lived and survived it—though maybe that's just me, through our shared Midwestern experience, or maybe he's just great at tapping into certain truths. Whatever else it might be, the poetry of an exposed nerve, a captured feeling in the lapse of a bleak moment, his work is the restless transcription of a personal myth.

I read *Witchita Stories* while standing, in a marathon of cigarette breaks on my front porch, back when I still smoked, and while the sky outside rained down hard across southwestern Portland. The book struck me instantly as something of a prelude to a masterpiece—the raw, confessional prose that's like a drunk, teary-eyed best friend finally letting you in on every terrible fucking thing that's ever happened to them. I was enthralled—and each story, like semi-healed scabs, started to peel me back through my own parallel time. Back toward when I didn't yet know that every death alters you some and a decade later you're someone you recognize less and less surrounded by a lot of ghosts. Toward two brothers I used to know when they were children, many years younger than I, now dead. The first, an overdose. He struggled with an addiction to opioids, later heroin. It would come out a year later that his older brother had shot up with him the night of his death. The brother's guilt would persuade him to take his own life in the same room a year later. This, and toward more dark things, toward moonless nights and cramped backseat nakedness, the unsolved disappearances in a small town's lore, and a suffocating wet Ohio heat as it all still exists in my head. That's what Weaver's writing does: it takes you back to your *There*.

Marigold almost didn't exist. This book had a different, less obvious title and was longer. Weaver and I nearly walked away from it. The book was only salvaged when, during an evening phone call in late December, we hashed out a plan to scrap most of it and start again. What you hold in your hands now is an earned "novel" forged from old pain. From its subject, an impulse inherent in all thinking creatures, to its terse execution, a setting and tone evocative in some ways of Harmony Korine and Breece D'J Pancake, one can imagine that the process of its creation involved a return to whatever boarded crawlspace birthed Weaver's prophetic voice in the first place. And I am immensely glad he survived to tell us about it. There are few, if any, wasted words within. I leave you now with the man himself.

Michael Kazepis
PORTLAND, 2016

The meaning of life is that it stops.

—FRANZ KAFKA

Marigold

Before I slip out of bed and slog to the bathroom, the first thing I do when I wake up in the morning is think, *Dammit, I woke up*, then fall back asleep for about ten minutes to give it another shot. Ten minutes later, I roll over, think, *Fuck it, I'm meant to be alive*—then the slipping, the slogging, the brushing, the shit, the shower, the shave. But before all that, before I even say words, before I scratch myself and roll out of bed, I stare at the glowing red numbers on the clock/radio and wonder where all the time has gone. Eight hours asleep every night for twenty-nine years. I'm only two-thirds alive. Not to mention all the napping that gets done on the weekends.

I dial up the suicide prevention hotline, get a busy signal, and wonder if that's a sign of the times.

This hair-twirling kid I work with is already texting me some bullshit about a band or something. It's 7:30 in the morning. I love Cocteau Twins just as much as anybody, but, *Come on, man, can't it wait?* I click the link with a yawn and listen to the song and stumble to the bathroom. Took a long time to end up me—utterly cynical and ready to die—and mister twirly-hair just doesn't get it. Sure, we may have a lot in common, but he has no idea just how fucked I truly am—and maybe I'm just as clueless.

Before the toothbrush scrapes across my teeth, before the shit, the shower, the shave, I stare into the mirror and think about how I'd like to go back to bed and give the whole not waking up thing another try. Then about how my little situation could be solved with a gun rack. Because if I had a gun rack, right above my bed, I'd have to someday get a gun to fit it—might wake up one day and not be so afraid to use it, if I had one. And say, if I had a blender, I'd make a margarita. Because, what the fuck else do you do with a blender? Can't shoot yourself through the face with that.

On the drive to work, I count the trashcans lining the curbsides like tombstones. So much trash, every single day, piling, crowding, till it becomes part of the landscape. Beautiful. There's so much I'd like to throw away, be done with, I think, then other times I think, *Fuck it, I'll be a hoarder. It's too easy to let go.* Then, *Shit, I forgot to take the can down to the curb again.* My home is a landfill. I don't even recycle.

Straining my eyes under a sagging gray headliner, I focus on the yellow stripes—artificial order. These lines keep us moving along with the herd, overtaking and passing them only to be overtaken and passed, always in realignment with the world. These lines point us toward our menial jobs, our stupid Wal-Marts. The true rebels, heroes to the causes of disorder and anarchy, are the martyrs who die in the easiest ways possible: accidentally. But who knows? I look down at the odometer, see I'm going ten over the limit, so I ease off the gas a bit, turn the radio up to drown my thoughts. I think I see a cop. Nope, just a white Ford Focus riding my ass. Garrison Keillor spews on about writers he has never read, three-cigarettes-burned-to-the-butt is a good unit of measure, I think, the gas light flashing red—and I know I'm there, my job. As soon as I see those red bricks, the shape of the building, I can only imagine a casket, shiny, black, towering indifferent to wants or needs. Other times I see the storm clouds. Maybe I'll take a sick day when I do it? That way I'm getting paid for it.

The dead speak to me through the mouths of the living—angry customers, each and every one of them. Because an iris or a lily didn't open in time for a funeral, because the shade of coral was the wrong shade of coral, because the dead can become unreasonable when they no longer can speak for themselves, I get called incompetent, get told I don't know how to do my job, and sometimes, worse than that, they say they'll come down to where I work and shove red roses up my ass.

The phone rings: *ring rrrrrrrrrrring.*
  "Hello . . . Hello? Helloooo?"
  "Mom, it's me . . ."
  Click.

Again, the living and the dead are just alike in most respects, interchangeable. Dead guy in a morgue or bride with a budget, they only like certain shades of flowers, deliberately difficult hues to match, all exotic and hard to find. On top of that, they want the expensive shit and have no money to buy it. Yet, tell them that. Just try and make a suggestion. I dare you. They tell you, *It's okay.* They'll try to be flexible. Flexible means shooting down every idea you come up with, every alternative, yet it doesn't do shit. Minds are made up. The dead and the living are just the same—same demands, same sadness, same fucking same thing.

The flowers make me sneeze, the sneeze clears me up, and I feel it, like, it's unpleasant and then it kicks with this incredible high—voltage through these plaqued-up veins. For a few seconds, I can breathe, I feel good, I'm alive and finally thankful. Shit-taking sometimes has the same effect. It's like throwing away the friends you thought you needed only for a spike on your stats chart, then waking up and realizing they threw you away, not vice versa. *I need to take the fucking trash out.*

Marigolds bloom from September to the first frost. Then they die and return to the soil, where they wait for the next September sun.

The guy in the corner who cuts the flowers is Hawaiian. Speaks pidgin. One time he told me, "Just listen to the first word and the last word, everything in between is meaningless." I've read so many books that've made me feel that way—*just meaningless.* He's a bad book, but he's an alright guy, doesn't mean he can't let you in, feel his presence, make him known. You don't have to read him. Just look. He's got this scar on his arm, near the crook, which is from the time he almost died, back in Hawaii, when he was in his mid-twenties. Punched his arm through a car window and yanked it out, left half a pound of meat on the asphalt, a few pints of blood at his feet. Said he saw the white light, like a pinpoint in the dark, and he kept reaching, just reaching out, because he knew he was almost home and that's the real struggle in this life.

This woman I work with will either die from skin cancer or a barbiturate overdose, that's the consensus. We're taking bets out back, during our smoke break. "I've got ten on cancer," says one. "Twenty says it's pills," says another. "She'll die in her sleep," I say, "I'll put twenty on it." But I know she won't die in her sleep. I just say it because that's what I want. It'll probably be some kind of cancer. It's always some kind of cancer.

Sun hails down on me like satanic proverbs from the mouth of Baphomet. I sweat into my eyes and say, "But fuck—masculinity is kissing bruised lips." Everyone is silent. The taller dude than me starts laughing. I say, "Masculinity is asking your mother for rent money then blowing it on a few cases of Bud Ice, some weed, and a box of condoms." Everyone starts laughing. I say, "Masculinity is jerking off to Monday night football." The laughter stops. "What the fuck, man," says the short guy.

Kid I work with twirls his hair like a methed-up banshee. We share a love for the same music and movies and art. Only problem here, he drives me crazy sometimes. Must be the age difference, makes things difficult—I'm almost thirty and he's just now twenty and going through his first breakup and how love feels and I'm just like, *Ugggg. Shut the fuck up.* I say this and other hurtful things, even though I know his pain, I know what it feels like when nobody wants to listen. But I don't know why I'm like this. He reminds me so much of myself at his age it makes me want to kill him.

A lot of the older men who come in and shop here are gay but married to women—some even have grown children. One time, I saw a man parked in a lurch at the park with that look of the hunt in his eyes. I can't imagine what that's like. They range from fifty to seventy years old. Times are different, things change—well, kind of they do. Recently, I noticed that one of them only hires hipsters in their early twenties to deliver flowers. Guess everything's a matter of taste. Though our motives are different, I commend him for his choice of hire. Sometimes I daydream about having conversations with these boys. *Fuck the Smashing Pumpkins! Let's talk about Cap'n Jazz and Big Black.* I think he likes them extra-smelly, too—like Dorito dust and three-weeks-worth of sweat collected in the cod of those tiny shorts.

10:30 AM. I'm letting loose in the bathroom, thinking about the show I watched on A&E last night. The serial killer Dean Corll was the subject. I'm thinking about Dean inserting glass tubes into his victim's urethras and then smashing their dicks with hammers while expelling my bowels, focusing on the floral print wallpaper, biting down on my lower lip, praying that come lunch time my rear driver-side tire is still holding its air.

For Want Of on repeat on my lunch break, in my car, not going anywhere, chain smoking, not eating because of the flat tire, draining my car's battery, relaxed but stressed, not dealing and watching cars drive by. Not eating, not moving, hardly breathing because it's easier to forget shit like that even matters sometimes.

Fifteen minutes left on my break, I dial up the hotline. I get Becky on the other end. Becky tries to sell me on how my life is worth living, even if sometimes it feels like it's not. I ask her what she had for lunch. "Ham and Swiss on rye," she says. "Just like Bukowski's childhood," I say. "Thanks, but no," I say. "I'd rather eat a short rope with a side of tears." She doesn't laugh like I do. She doesn't laugh at all. It's just so easy not to laugh sometimes, people taking things so seriously.

A sixty-plus grump with a humor problem comes waltzing over to give me some shit. I say, "Hey, how've you been?" His face sags, old and ugly, and he says, "Terrible, just terrible." I say, "What's wrong?" He says, "Your face, that's what. Your face, it's just all wrong." I grin. I say, "Well, yours, your face, it's beautiful, something to behold." He frowns and grunts and hobbles into the cooler to be a dick to the flowers he'll soon lay over a grave in the countryside.

When I started this job I was a driver, drove something like four-hundred miles a day, five days a week. I did this for two and a half years. We'd start at six in the morning, getting off at four-thirty or five. Driving all day alone wears on you after a while. I started talking to myself. Then the tears only severe isolation can bring. I started punching myself in the face so I wouldn't fall asleep at the wheel and kill somebody. Another trick for not killing anyone is drinking a ton of coffee and when it's time to piss, just hold it and drink some more. The darker the better. You'll never fall asleep like that, I'll guarantee it.

Hair twirling kid comes up to me and says, "I don't know. I just don't understand why she won't talk to me." I look him in the eyes and say, "She doesn't want to talk to you. She doesn't want anything to do with you. You dumped her. Get over yourself. Move on." I mean every word of it, too, even though I immediately want to take it back. I want to say, "The world's a good place. People are kind. People are inherently good. There is nothing wrong with either one of you. Just some bad chemistry. The world is full of possibilities. Stop selling yourself short all the time. Also, that music you listen to—listen to something happier, like Xiu Xiu." But I don't. I just stick with the first, because there never seems to be enough time for the second.

Reticence is a word I think of often, I'm just not sure how to use it. It's constantly at the tip of my tongue, teetering back and forth, folding in on the sound of itself.

Marigolds are pollinated by beetles and flies, and they contain hermaphroditic florets.

The lady I work with who will die of cancer, she's got these cans on her and likes to get up real close to me and heave her lungs out so I'll take a lonesome peek at that breathing vision. It makes me uncomfortable, even though I always look, and wonder about what my wife would think of me. If I back away, she'll inch closer. I don't know what's worse, the sexual discomfort or her bad breath. Neither is very pleasant. Nothing seems worth whatever it is she's offering.

The feeling gets stronger every year, from way back to the time I struck out in Tee Ball. I was eight years old. Now and again there's a swirling above me, a forming, like clouds, and I go back to that swing, that miss, the humiliation—both sad and glad my father never made it to a single game.

The little Hawaiian guy missed work one time because he had a sty and didn't want people to notice his eye being watery. *I don't want them to think I'm a little bitch*, he said. All I could think was, *Masculinity is missing work.*

Edouard Leve killed himself ten days after turning in his final manuscript. The manuscript was titled *Suicide*. Sometimes I think that's badass and other times I think that's so sad. Sometimes I think I would like to do something similar. I'll title mine *Birth, Rebirth, Afterbirth*. I'll be late to work forever.

Between the ages of eight until, well, now, I use to check myself for cancer—my balls, my lymph-matter: armpits, groin, neck, all over—and now, now I just ignore any pains or discomfort or ticks my body complains about. Just roll with it, that's my motto. Like this weird red mole that just popped up on my chest. Melanoma? Who the fuck knows?

Needles are the worst, the absolute no, the main reason I never go for checkups. The only motherfucker taller than me at work, by maybe an inch, the part-timer, he sells plasma twice a week. Has the track marks to prove it. So, needles? *No.* They aren't even a distraction or a problem for him. Just an annoyance. I mean, is it the same thing? What I mean is, does poverty make it easier to get used to needles? Is there that much separation between taking blood and injecting a drug, to compensate? Drawing blood, poisoning it. All these people that worship the same gods, things they can hold or which hold them back, if only fleetingly—none of them can see it's all the same face if you look hard enough—these gods, these people, these lives . . .

The overweight black dude, maybe my favorite person in the world, who drives all the way to Dodge City and back every day, comes up to me while I'm packing a hundred red roses delicately into a cardboard box and he says, "What if I took this knife and slit my throat, right in front of you, looking you in the eyes while the blood spurts out of me and onto your face?" I laugh and think *great idea, give me that matador confetti,* but then, all serious-like, I look him in the eyes, and say, "Well, to be honest, I'd be fucking devastated!" He laughs, says, "Good answer," and then he proceeds to tell me what position he fucked his wife in last night, in what room, under what circumstances. The kids were in the backyard playing with some firecrackers. "I stared at the wall and imagined cute things dying so I wouldn't cum too soon."

When I listen to Souvlaki by Slowdive, I feel alright about things for a while. The sadness, the melancholy, it all makes me smile. I find it funny, too, my reaction, because a lot of people tell me that album makes them feel suicidal.

Watched a show about Fatty Arbuckle last night and, today, while I'm talking to some dude on the phone about some precious wedding he needs flowers for, all I can think of is a champagne bottle and a butthole, his butthole, and all the aftermath with the blood and the public, how my life might have been better if I'd just stuck with my instincts and ate myself and drank myself and fucked myself to death, let the blood from my veins out onto the bathroom floor when I was eight because *who the fuck strikes out in Tee Ball?*

An hour from closing up shop, the phone rings and rings and rings. I'm already on the line with a customer, but I say, *Hold it a sec there, would you, Barb? The assholes I work with won't pick up the other line.* I look at them, each and every one of them, six all counted, and realize they are all either on the phones with customers or with customers who have come into the store. I look down at both of my hands. They're empty. I don't wear a headset. I must have been daydreaming. I mutter something under my breath, but it's so silent, what I'm saying, and I'm so zoned-out, I don't even know what it is that so offends everybody.

When I'm hopeless, I feel alive. The pressure is great. We all have choices. Choices are dangerous. I hope I make the right one.

I call the hotline and get someone named Sandra. I ask to speak with Becky. She tells me that Becky is no longer with them. I hang up the phone and stare out at the city passing me by, just blurs of green and grey with no distinction.

When I get home and see my wife, things go warm, and everything that came before recedes. We drive to Starbucks. We eat horrible food for dinner. We play with the dogs. We argue about mundane things. We watch Seinfeld. We go to bed then she falls asleep. She snores. I sleep with a smile on my face, even knowing the hell to come from the ordinary the moment the alarms sound. I sleep and I dream. I never remember my dreams, but I know that I'm dreaming. Someone once told me the moment you stop dreaming is the moment you're no longer alive. Isn't that something?

"Is Sandra there?" I ask someone named Jose. He tells me she doesn't work at this particular call center, but people are very fond of Sandra and he can patch me through if I'd be willing to hold. "Hold," I say, "hold away. But make it snappy, please."

An hour later, I'm still on hold, still thinking about my head Plath-style in the oven, still thinking about whether or not it will be painless like they say it is. I'm scared of the pain, that's my main problem. I'm scared to feel things. Anything. I mean, what if I like it, the feeling of dying, what if the pain makes me happy and it's already too late for realizations, because by the time I start feeling it, the pain, and liking it, I'll be too dead to save myself from myself? Think about it. Then I wouldn't be able to live in the pain best suited to my spirit. I wouldn't be able to admire and enjoy my invention of comfort, wouldn't be able to sleep on the rocks I'll soon call pillows. Finally, I hang up and think, *Fuck, I could've killed myself at least thirteen times by now.*

Next day at work, hair-twirling kid's not there. Everyone looks sad. Cancer lady is talking to tall guy and they both have tears in their eyes. *What in the fuck is happening?* And I get it, the news: he shot himself through the head last night. I go outside and smoke cigarettes, trying to come to terms with it. He was more than a hair-twirling coworker, he was a human being. He was my friend. I mean, I'm so fucking sad I can't even think. I fumble for my cellphone, wanting to know what people may or may not be saying on social media, needing a little more information. I pull my phone out of my pocket, and see I have two new text messages. Both are from him, the almighty hair-twirling wonder. First one reads: *I really need somebody to talk to.* And the second one: *When you get this, please call me.* I can't breathe. I smoke faster, take bigger drags, hold the smoke in longer, try to hold it in so long I feel my brain cells start fizzling out like sparklers. In four days there will be a funeral. I'll see him then, one last time. I wonder if we'll be providing the flowers for his visitation.

What is the best way to die? I answer myself with mute moving lips. I wake up in a sweat, tears in my eyes. I'm so fucking sad I think I'll go up to that hair-twirling fucker and punch him right in his stupid gut tomorrow. Nightmare inducing bastard, that kid. I'll go up to him and say, "I thought you were dead! You asshole! I thought you were dead!"

My wife, beautiful and wondering, contemplates each passage in a book about saints as she reads aloud to me in our basement. I stopped paying attention after Saint Appollonia, who wore a gold tooth around her neck or some shit, and I wondered what she looked like when she ate, before she was a martyr, gold tooth and all, before we gave the world its veins with plastic plumbing. The image in my head is miraculous, an incomplete painting, an erasure, actually—only a tooth, gold-fading, hovering in the ether of some bloody gums in a sinew-wrapped skull. And I can't see enough of it—I'm trying to see it, as I write these words. I can't. My imagination is shot. No pictures to be drawn.

Marigold florets are often mixed with chicken feed. Makes the yolks a brighter yellow, I'm told, for those who care for such things.

After work one day, I buy bullets for a .22. My best friend has one hidden in his closet. I've shot targets with it. I'm a shitty aim, but I'm pretty sure I can't miss my own head. It would be worse than the Tee Ball thing if I missed my own head. I'd have to stay alive just to live with myself. That would be my punishment. I made sure to keep the receipt, you know, just in case.

The hours spill like shadows across the day. It's three going on four going on seven, feels like the longest 8th inning stretch I've never witnessed. I'm watching my corners, waiting for the bums to come out and pester me for change. Recently, I've been all along this road and they're always there, nagging my conscience with their patient eyes, like this one bag lady I met last Tuesday. Her name is Allison. She came at me out of nowhere and only for a quarter to call her sister back in Delaware. I thought, *Delaware? My god, how far you've come.* The soles on her shoes flapped up and down like sad, cartoon lips. I told her I'd give her a quarter if she'd join me for a cup of coffee after she used the phone. She shook her head, saying, "Nah, coffee ain't a thing." I knew, I already knew it—what she wanted. "Let me guess," I said. "You'd rather have a beer, wouldn't you?" And instantly, I felt sorry I'd said it. These old lips are best left closed. But she didn't take offense, not at all. She just said, "Actually, I just was thinking I could use a shower. You live close by?" This was the moment her beauty showed its hand. See, I'd misgauged her age by at least fifteen years and was just then noticing what lie beneath my first impressions, because she held her head up for the first time to me and then smiled this smile that said, *Just get me to a fucking bathroom so I can show you I'm a lot more than all this dirt on my skin.*

It only strikes me later that quarter-to-use payphones are obsolete.

I take her to my place for a shower. She is in there about thirty, forty-five minutes. I put her clothes in the wash and wait. When she comes out, she looks amazing, like you wouldn't even believe. We watch Seinfeld reruns while her clothes dry. My wife comes home, startled and uncomprehending, this strange woman sitting on the couch in her bathrobe, and starts with this look and aggressive wave of the hand.

"And who is this?"

"This," I say. "This—this is . . ."

"Allison," says Allison, and she sticks her hand out for a shake, but my wife, she just looks at it, turns around and leaves the house.

"Well," I say, "how about that beer?"

The short walk home must feel like the longest distance when you live in the street.

I dial up the hotline, get a dude named Matt. I tell Matt I'd like to ask him a question. Matt says, "Shoot, ask me anything." All the sudden there is this horrible swollen feeling in my chest. I go silent. Matt says, "Hello? Hello? Are you there?" I can't choke through the throat-fucked feeling to say, *Yes, Matt. Yes, I am. I'm here.* I hang up the phone and swallow back the bile, wipe the tears from my cheeks, and go into the kitchen to eat a hotdog with mustard.

After I wash the last dog chunk down with orange soda, I patch things up with my wife—explain the whole why-I-had-a-homeless-woman-on-the-couch-watching-Seinfeld thing. She says she understands, she thinks I'm a good man and all that you-have-such-a-big-heart stuff, but I sense something in her tone, like she only half-believes my story or something, and, for the moment, I'm okay with that.

I think of the taller dude at work, how he said he use to ride miniature bulls back when he was nine or ten. Rodeo for children—he loved it. Then, one day, they wanted him to ride the big bull, not the mini, and he wasn't about it. That was the end of his bull-riding career. But he talked and talked about all the pussy he was getting from riding on the minis. At first, I was like, *Oh, yeah, well, good for you, man.* But then I was like, *Wait a second, didn't you say you were nine or ten.* He looked nervous, but he laughed, then I laughed, and then we were both laughing so hard we were unable to stop. I was crying. Then our boss came out of his office. Said, *What's so funny? What're you guys laughing about?* We looked at each other, looked back at our boss, and said, *Nothing, just this stupid thing. Don't worry about it.* For the rest of the day, we did the eggshell walk, even while taking the trash out. At the dumpster, dumping the cans, I wondered what it would be like to crawl inside one and take a nap. A few years back, a homeless man died that way. Fell asleep in a dumpster at the mall one cold winter night and got compacted in the trash truck. Truck was too loud to hear his screams. Life feels like that sometimes, doesn't it? Like a scream that gets muffled by the crushing.

The streetlights blink from green to yellow to red, all the spaces between—it's all so fucking loud. Red tells you to stop, and at night it spills across the ground like puddles of blood with no sun for a straw—stained and ugly in the moonlight.

Dunkelheit.

My wife and I go to the zoo and gaze at the beautiful animals behind their glass and bars and slats and shadows. An overweight teenager is selling popcorn and cotton candy—there are refreshments and t-shirts and balloon animals. *You want a Coke?* I say, I'm sold. My wife says she'd like Coke. While I'm at it I grab a bag of butter-smothered popcorn. While we eat, we watch the chimpanzees fling their shit at the glass right in front of us, which, I notice, tends to lend a more appropriate tinge to my reflection.

We feed the Koi hard brown pellets that resemble goat turds. I've always wanted to live under water.

I'm watching atrocity footage on Youtube on my lunchbreak when my overweight black friend comes into the break room and says, "Man, how can you watch this shit?" "Easy," I say. "It makes me feel like I'm making an effort to truly be connected to the world." I don't know what I mean by saying this and, clearly, neither does he—he's all blank stares and shoulder shrugs. "Well," he says, "you know what I say. Get rid of it, all of it, the footage, the history, you know, so that it doesn't end up repeating itself." I shake my head. "I think the point is to keep it alive in the archives so that it doesn't repeat itself," I say, but I don't know what it is I really think, I just say it. I don't know, maybe he has a point? Everybody has a point, whether it's a bullshit point or not—points are points. But maybe he has a truth deeper than the truths in my heart—I'm just too whitewashed to see it.

I scribble on my napkin a poem:

Gay alligator wrestlers in leotards paint my dreams in argyle. But no, I'm fucking printed in scales. Spread my legs and fly away, dick bag. I'll wrestle a gay alligator to his death, but I won't wrestle you, you fucking cheat. I've got scales and a nine. I'm talking dick, not cal., bitch, so fucking bring it with the skin machine.

Cross it out.

Throw it away.

Wonder what it tells me about myself tomorrow.

Tomorrow is Monday. I know there's another poem in there, another thought I'd like to end, another thing I don't like about myself revealed:

Monday again, perpetual mind-death, and here I am

Taking the last jelly donut and thinking "who fucking

cares if it's the last one? There will always be more."

But I'm terrible at poems and even worse at living.

Guess that's why I go out on lunch to my car so my

Friends can find me there just that much closer to death

But nope, not dead, I'm all donut-breath and sleeping.

I crumple up the shitty poem and stuff it into my back pocket, listen for the phone to ring. It doesn't. I need somebody to need me for more than what I'm selling. More than anything, I want to spill my soul to a perfect stranger who actually gives a shit, just to know what that might feel like.

If I were to spill my soul, it would resemble this ink. If I were to spill my blood, it would resemble this ink. If I were to spill this ink, it would resemble this ink, but this ink formed into shapes and textures, letters and numbers and symbols, and they'd become part of you, like an infection.

Note to my wife: I want to fill shotgun shells with tiny paper hearts and shoot them into your chest.

Note to my wife: When I wake in the morning, and I'm frustrated I'm still alive, sometimes the only thing that gets me out of bed is: knowing you'll be right back in that same bed when the day is done. Sometimes it's hard, sometimes not so much, and sometimes I forget I even exist—you're everything. It's like sleep walking. These are the worst, the sleep-walk days—like, *Kill me, please.* This morning, though, it was easy. I saw your face there beside me, floating above your vacant pillow, and I said *I love you* to the wall.

I go over to my best friend's and sneak into his closet. I pull out the little .22 handgun he has tucked under some shoes. Put it in my mouth and pull the trigger. Nothing happens. I'm not even scared. I pull it again, nothing, wipe my spit from the barrel and put it back. I walk back out into the living room. They're singing the last lines of Happy Birthday. I'm late to the party. But the baby, it's a healthy first birthday. I smile and watch as everybody who's of age gorges on food and beer, while the infant stupidly stares at a lightbulb. Drawn there like a moth.

Mom calls on my lunchbreak.

"Hello?"

"Hey, how's my son?"

"Good. How're you? How's dad?"

"Dad's been struggling, but, overall, he's good. He sure does miss you."

"I miss him too—I love you, mom."

"I love you too, sweetie."

"So what kind of trouble you two been getting into lately?"

"Well, not a whole lot. Just sitting around—retirement makes you lazy."

"Not lazy, mom, just stagnant. Not a whole lot going on, anyway. Why leave the house?"

"We need to, that's why. We need to do stuff. We just sit here all day and rot away, watching Fox and old movies your dad likes."

"Well, I mean, you guys don't really get around like you use to."

"Oh, we do just fine! We aren't old."

"No, that's not what I meant. Sorry. I just want you to be happy, mom, really."

"I'm happy enough."

"Is dad happy?"

"He's happy enough."

"Well, okay."

"What're you getting at?"

"Nothing. I'm not getting at anything."

The phone dies.

I think about the wars being waged in this world. I want to know what it feels like to have a bullet through the heart. A bullet filled with hate. I want to know death, the kind of feeling that forgives the murderer before the trigger's even pulled.

I call up the hotline, hang up, and immediately start to cry.

Savage Arms shotgun, serial #B366615—Breece D'J Pancake exited the world in the thunderclap of that blast. But his words, those perfect little ghosts, his words, they will live forever. And so will his bones. A million years down and curious kids will find his fossils encrusted in the side of the earth's shoulder blades. They'll make necklaces out of his teeth, marveling over the molars, and carve the word "heart" into each and every rib bone.

Antonin Artaud should've killed himself. He would've been a much happier man. Ten years a slave.

I walk out to my car at the end of the day. I think about what we are and what we aren't—mercenaries, citizens, people. We all act like we acted when we were too drunk and stupid to care, when we were in high school and college. We do. *We still do this,* I think. The entire world is filled with teenagers.

Drinking forties and hopping trains, beating the shit out of parked cars with baseball bats, walking out of the bowling alley with the rental shoes still on, smoking weed while the others smoke meth and poke themselves with needles, inject, whatever, and all of us feeling like this is what we are supposed to do with ourselves on a boring Sunday night. Drinking and driving and puking on ourselves in the snow, making angel prints with our dirty bodies—blowing smoke rings with our stinky breath. Carving the initials of the girls we have crushes on into our leg meat, hoping when it scars it'll look super cool and that it'll maybe even land the girl for a burger and a fuck. Funneling box wine down our gullets, slugging each other in the head, face, stomach, neck, and eating fried food from our laps, like nothing much matters but the French fries and the dipping sauces, even when the sky has spread its legs wide and birthed a billion stars, which are burning bright as seared coals outside the city limits. Putting our hand up her shirt and sucking the lipstick off her lips, tasting the swill of her slightly buzzed saliva, hardening in our pants, our dicks, collective façades and machismos, yet feeling the fear that comes with getting to know somebody better, you know, like that, anyway, investigatory, and wondering where that strange sound is coming from, seemingly lost and sucked up in the darkness of the woods. Feeling the ticks sink into the skin behind our ears, wondering if that isn't the sound we hear in the distance. Worrying about Lyme disease while drunk-trickling into the condom come the dark swirling intensity of her orgasm, while she's clenching hold of our butt cheeks, both hands, making us feel like we'll never escape the grip, and praying she never lets go of any single one of us. She's my home, my city, my state, my heart in the middle of the country, and we are too fucked up to even remember the beautiful moments, let alone the desperate ones. We try, don't we? We fail, don't we? We fuck you with our middle fingers, bring you to your knees with a few flicks of the wrist. But you've forgotten us, left us to rot in your denial, our denial, and denial is what we live for. Deny me, deny us, deny this, but don't deny yourself. But you can and you will. You deny

that denial is a stain in your reflection, same as me.
Hardly even here to begin with.

Memories always take place in the present tense.

The woman who will die from cancer, she won't die from cancer, she won't die from anything, not at all, as long as I know her name and keep it. She's a good woman with a good head on her shoulders. Hard-working and loose with her tongue, she comes up to me at the grocery store, gives me a big hard hug and says, "You and your lady should come over later. We're going to be grilling in the back yard." I tell her we'll be there and continue on with my purchases. When I get home, I don't even tell my wife about it. I ignore the fact that we've been invited to do something for once. I spend all afternoon Facebooking while occasionally glancing at stupid reality shows flash across the TV screen, more surreal and eerie than anything.

Halloween party just the two of us, and things are rocky. *Frisk me later,* she says, *I'll take a raincheck.* She leaves abruptly, saying, Fuck you—paisley wallpaper and a lusty desire to leave this room/stay here forever drowns me, shrouds me in a black cloud of shit-memory. The smell, her smell, is all over me, austere and sweet, and even though she stopped four tugs too short, I know she loves me. It's Halloween and my face is painted like those dudes in Black Metal bands. Skull on flesh, inside out, the way it should be, showing only the core, indistinguishable from the other skeletons—here, now, always, your servant soon covered in dirt.

I take the dogs out back so they can hike up and pee on their pissing-bush. I dial up the hotline, get someone named Alexander. "Alexander," I say. "How are you doing today?"

"I'm okay. How are you?"

"Just okay?" I say. "There's a tone in your voice. It doesn't settle well with me. I don't think you're doing as 'okay' as you think you are—you want to talk about it?"

"What?" says Alexander, a little bit of a crack in his voice, then there's silence.

"Alexander? You still there, bud?"

I hear him take a couple of breaths.

"Alexander? You all right, man?"

He hangs up and I stamp my cigarette out against the shed and take the dogs back into the house. My wife won't be home until seven. I call back and ask for Alexander. They won't give me Alexander. I hang up my phone and consider getting more beer. I'll probably need more beer.

I get more beer.

The cold bites at my face as I walk downtown to where all the homeless congregate. I'm looking all through the crowds trying to zero in on a face, any face, but one that's familiar. A few times I start to jog towards someone, only to find a bearded man or a frozen child there in my grip, not resembling the face I'm searching for. Other times I think I hear a familiar voice and try to follow its lilt, but the words warp in the wind and change direction, get lost in the alleys and the trees and the fading light.

Marigolds emit oils which smell something awful. Because of this, Marigolds are often planted next to other crops, such as tomatoes, because the noxious oils keep insects away. Wonder if they keep the worms away? If so, plant some over my grave.

How is it I get here every waking day?

I think of my overweight black friend from work. *What if I took this knife and slit my throat, right in front of you, looking you in the eyes while the blood spurts out of me and onto your face?*

Well, I think, *I'd grab a bucket and fill it so I could put it all back into you.*

I call the hotline and ask for Ida. I've never talked to an Ida before, but I figure it's worth a shot. It takes ten seconds before they connect me. It's a lady named Ida and she sounds about my mom's age.

Idea for a painting: Edouard Manet's *The Suicide* and Edouard Leve's *Suicide* side by side with a box of shells, a shotgun, and a quartered apple on a messy bed.

The hair-twirler's been having more problems lately, tells me he needs to see a shrink and get on meds, tells me it is okay if he's a little fucked-up as long as he's seeking help. I say, "Damn right, man. Get all the help you can. You already know it, but, you know, I can't help you. I can't even help myself."

Rope.
Razor.
Gas.
Gun.
Poetry.
Capitalism.

Sometimes we are our own cancer. It's a faster kind, more aggressive. I want that boldness so bad sometimes I can't even see what I'll miss.

My phone vibrates softly in my pocket. I ignore it. I'm jerking off. She's quite a distance off, but I'm closing in, closer, closer, closer. My phone vibrates. Again, I ignore it. I continue in pursuit of orgasm. It vibrates again. I jizz on the tiles. Somebody needs me. I text back: *Sorry, I'm busy. Can I call you later?* I don't even see who it is, and have no intention of calling them back. My life has come to this. I'm an asshole. I hate myself and I want to die.

I go get some soda on foot. The walk home from the gas station feels like treading water, but when I get there, there's a hot dinner on the table, and the smiling face of the love of my life, the woman I married six short years ago, asks me if I've heard from the kid I work with who twirls his hair. "No," I say. "Why? Everything all right?" She clicks her fork against her teeth. "You know how he is," she says. "He kept texting me while I was at work. Just saying the usual stuff, you know—My life SUCKS—I feel like dying—I H8 EVERYTHING. You know— the usual. I tried to comfort him the best I could, but, after a while, it just gets to going in circles, you know." I nod. "I know," I say. "He's so exhausting at times."

Some ugly girl walks into work and the taller dude nudges me and says, *"You can have her."* I nudge him back, "You're such an asshole." He laughs. I look at him, I mean, seriously look at him, to let him know that I'm disappointed. He kind of does this frown maneuver with his jaw then he lets out this half laugh/half burp, and takes off toward the bathroom. I'd like to know what the hell it is he does in there for thirty minutes every day after lunch. When he comes out, he looks sweaty and red, and he comes up and says, "So for real, though, you're seriously checking out that Buddha bitch?"

I call my brother and tell him I'm pretty sure I'm ready to die. He thinks I'm just kidding around or something, because all he does is laugh and says, "Shit, I know the feeling, bro. Life." I tell him that I'd like my death to be interpreted as a eulogy to the American Dream. And that I want everybody to light a birthday candle and make the world burn bright for a future wish. "Hopefully someone out there has strong enough lungs to blow them out— make the wish come true," he says. And here's my wish. Sometimes I wish he'd just know the right things to say to me. But who ever does? You know?

Pretty sure my brother tried to pierce his dick with a safety pin one time, same as he did with his left nipple. That or his girlfriend was wearing his tighty-whiteys and had some leakage during her period. Or maybe the underwear was right there in the attic before the house was built in a different dimension in space and time? Things are so strange sometimes you could almost say everything and anything is true. Nothing is false. Truth. We are all TV commercials, sitcoms, news tickers—we are the denial that we're any of those things. Nature doesn't even exist. At least I haven't seen any proof of it, if it does. But it's true, one time I found bloody underwear in our attic. Sometimes, I wake in the morning with the underwear image right there in front of me, and there's a smell to it, too, but I don't know what it is.

My wife calls me on her lunch break in a panic. Says we can't afford to pay our bills. Says I should start considering getting a second job. I tell her I should be on pills or in therapy. *Growing up in my family gave me PTSD*, I say. Then I remember when I was in therapy in my early teens, my therapist wanted me to write about my childhood experiences. I wrote only once. I wrote this thing about my neighborhood and shit, the kids and the trouble and the kids.

Sam's the short kid, the one always sporting bloody lips. He can't keep his mouth shut. Bill's Sam's older brother. He's blonde and popular and has muscles. Rumor has it he fucked a twenty-year-old on his twelfth birthday. But that's the past. Now Sarah is Bill's girlfriend. Sarah has a body like the mannequins at the mall. I always get semi-erect when I walk past those mannequins. Everything's tight, petite, almost doesn't seem a healthy weight, but they're sure as shit beautiful, plastic or flesh. Sarah gives me a picture of her in her cheerleading outfit, and tells me to think about her sometime while jerking off. I laugh and pretend not to hear her, and stuff the picture into my front pocket, hoping my penis grazes it as I walk. And I know, right then, she'll stick with me for many years to come. I'm a year older than the other three, but I'm three years younger than Carlos, the Mexican dude who rolls the meanest joints I've ever seen. Countless times we've smoked with Carlos. Countless times he tells us how the world is falling apart. Not how, but about how, you feel me? Carlos has a sister Sam's interested in, but we all know how that will end up so we keep telling him to just go get another girl, somebody older, somebody who can live with the bullshit shit-talk and the bloody lips. Sam doesn't hear a thing, he never has, and so he keeps insisting she's the one, she's the girl he has to have. Celia. Celia's a real beauty, though, there's no doubt about that, but still, he needs to get somebody more on his level, somebody who can take his abuse. I don't know. My little brother thinks I'm a disappointment ever since I started smoking. I'm trying, though. I really am. Maybe if I hook him and Sarah up and get Bill with Celia, he'll forgive me. At least it would fix the whole Sam/Celia problem. Plus, Carlos loves Bill. He doesn't mind Sam, but he doesn't really like him either, you feel me? It isn't easy for us, none of us. But let me just say this. Sarah's a beast. She really is. Sometimes, if I concentrate hard enough, I can get going to the rhythm of her heartbeat. And all the others, all of them, they just stand around not even knowing, watching from the distance as my daddy's brown Buick rocks in the side street.

My first fiction, my first lie, my first truth.

The lady I work with who will no longer die of cancer texts me out of the blue—asks if I can meet her at her mechanic's in the morning, before we go to work. I type out some words and quickly erase them. I do it again. Erase. I put my phone in my pocket and fall asleep. I wake up in the morning, feeling shittier than ever. I text her: *Still need me to meet you at the shop?* She texts back: *Thanks, but I worked it out with someone else.* I roll over in my bed, stare at the red glare of numbers telling me to get up, get ready, and start the day. *You can't afford to be late again,* I say. That gun rack seems like a better idea than ever. So does the gun to fit it. And the blender? Yeah, this all sounds like a trip to paradise.

On the drive to work, they're talking to Norman Mailer on NPR. He answers every question with a smugness that could make a person puke. Just masturbation, the words coming out of that man, the world we live in—a place which deliberately celebrates this particular brand of evil.

When I die, maybe they'll harvest the flowers that grow from my corpse and plant them in a vase, in a house, on a mantle, where they'll receive no sunlight and wither to dust, inevitably choking someone up as they pass me by. My only hope is that they'll spit me back out into the soil to become one with the flowers.

The taller motherfucker than me, he says we should just go over to the Middle East and *kill all of them "Mozlums"—I mean, show them absolutely no fucking mercy.* I tell him he's worse than an idiot, he's a patriot, a Fox News parrot, a nationalist, a shitslinging bigot. And then I think of all the moments I've had with customers who say shitty, racist things, like, they think I'm just going to somehow miraculously agree with them. And guess what? I do, I fucking agree with them—keeping in mind, of course, when I agree with somebody I'm usually lying. Can't close the sale if you actually show these people you're a different kind of human being.

But I'm not. I'm no different than them, that's just it. I'm just me and they're just them and we are all just this lump of clutter stuck here together, we just don't navigate in the same ways—that's the only difference. It's all so very true and simple and so vaguely wrong and misguided at the same time, the way I think. We're all pretty much the same give or take a few pounds—that's it. The other things, the things that pit us against each other, that's the disease speaking—the consequence of being human.

You can't kill yourself if you're only just pretending to live.

After work, my wife and I invite hair-twirling kid over to drink beer with us in our basement. I worry about him a lot. He's just like this aimless young dude who snorts coke on the weekends, whatever, but I feel a real sense of something close with him—I don't know. I want to kill him and yet I want to hug him and tell him that everything's going to be fine. I don't want to lie, though, that's the thing. I lie all day long for my job. If you consider putting up with bullshit comments all day lying, I'm in it to win it. But lie to a friend? Come on.

He comes in through the back door, hair-twirling and semi-crazy, carrying a six-pack of some rotgut, says, "Hi, honeys, I'm home!"

Immediately I feel like punching him the face, but I say, "Hey, man, how's it going? Looking good, looking good. What do you got there, man?"

"PBR," he says.

We talk about bullshit and bullshit and more bullshit. Finally I stand up and say, "What the fuck is up with all this bullshit, man? Tell me something anybody in the world gives a shit about and then we can talk."

"What the fuck, man?" he says. "Alright, I'm sorry, I'm sorry."

"Well, fucker, you should be sorry," I say. "Because, you know what, you are looking into a fucking mirror right now and you're hell of a lot better than your reflection."

I dial up the hotline and get Marge. Marge tells me more about herself than the others do. Tells me about her husband and her kids and the church she attends. I say, "But Marge, I know life can be beautiful, it's just not beautiful for me. I don't think I was meant to be alive." And she says, "Well, you know, that may or may not be the case, but the thing is, the thing to remember is, we, all of us, we are what we've done, nothing more, nothing less. Now, what do you want to be? Remembered or forgotten? It's up to you. I'm just here to tell you there are options. Living another day is the best death you could ask for."

I call my wife just to tell her I love her. She doesn't answer. I tell her voicemail that I love it instead.

Hawaiian guy who cuts the flowers, he tells me how much lobster he had over the weekend, how many beers he drank, what it felt like when he smoked that big-ass blunt and rear-fucked his chick. I act like I'm interested in all of it, nodding and even laughing occasionally, and then he starts in on his bitching about having to pay child support. I pull my cellphone out of my pocket and pretend to take a call. He gets the message and goes and shares the same information with hair-twirling kid. It's like, *Man, I have my own problems . . . and yours aren't all that fucking entertaining or different than mine. Still, though, I consider you a friend. We have that in common.*

Consider the Lobster

Consider the receipt in my pocket. Consider the gun that isn't mine to use. Consider the life that is mine that isn't mine to take. Consider consideration itself.

Hair-twirling kid calls me, says, "I've got a gun against my temple." I say, "Cool, man, me too." He says, "I'm not joking. I'm done. I'm fucking done," and he starts crying. I try to sound concerned, "Put the gun down, man. Sure, life can be shitty. I get it. I know. But what's even shittier is giving up, you know, like who knows, maybe you'll be the dude who finds the cure for cancer or whatever." I feel like a hypocrite. I am a hypocrite. I imagine his bullet tunneling instead through my own frontal lobe, a forever lobotomy—death showering warmth and light over me. I say, "Dude, cut the shit. Get that fucking gun out of your fucking face or so help me god . . . I'll . . ." and suddenly I'm crying, too, and we are in this immense moment of existential togetherness, astray in the wilderness of being, but hand in hand. After a few minutes, he says, "Damn, dude, are *you* okay?" I say, "No, I'm not fucking okay." Silence. "Put the gun down," I say, "and I'll tell you a secret." He says, "Okay," and I can hear some shuffling. "Okay," I say, "listen closely. You want to know the best way to kill yourself?" He sniffs, says, "Yeah." "That's good. I'll tell you tomorrow."

Thanks can and must and will always go to: Kevin Sampsell, J David Osborne, Michael Kazepis, Wendy Ortiz, Jamie Iredell, Sean H. Doyle, Michael Seidlinger, Brian Alan Ellis, Scott Mc-Clanahan, Juliet Escoria, Mike Young, Jac Jemc, Peter Markus, Nat Baldwin, Sam Wilson, Ken Baumann, Blake Butler, J Ryan Stradal, Michael Bible, Kevin Maloney, Elizabeth, Jane, Peter, Madelyn, Fran, Randy, Chad, Paul, Amanda, Mom, Dad, and Preston. Much love and gratitude to every single one of you.

Thank you for picking up this King Shot Press title. We are a small press based in Portland, Oregon, dedicated to the publication of fine works of prose and poetry. If you loved reading the book you hold in your hands, do please tell your friends about it. For more information about us, see www.kingshotpress.com.

Also Available from King Shot Press

Leverage by Eric Nelson
Strategies Against Nature by Cody Goodfellow
Killer &Victim by Chris Lambert
Noctuidae by Scott Nicolay
I Miss The World by Violet LeVoit

Troy James Weaver is the author of *Witchita Stories* and *Visions*. His work has appeared in *The Nervous Breakdown*, *The LitHub*, *Heavy Feather Review*, *NAILED MAGAZINE*, *Vol. 1 Brooklyn*, and a few other places, both online and in print. He lives in Wichita, Kansas with his wife, two dogs, and nephew.